This book belongs to:

the AMAZING SPIDER-MAN

The Big Top Mystery

by David Anthony Kraft
Marie Severin
Earl Norem

MARVEL BOOKS

Peter Parker is a very smart science student. One day, he went to a very interesting science demonstration. Little did he realize that the experiment in radiation would change his life forever!

For, unknown to anyone, a small spider was hit by a beam of radiation. And that spider fell on Peter and bit him on the hand!

The bite from the radioactive spider suddenly gave Peter super-human strength! And, he could crawl on walls — just like a spider! He made himself some special web-shooters and a costume and became the Super-Hero known as Spider-Man!

One day, Peter and his Aunt May went to the circus.

"I love circuses," says Aunt May. "And this one is owned by a dear friend of mine, Brad Steel!"

"I remember you talking about him!" says Peter. "He's really famous!"

"Why, it's May and Peter!" shouts Brad, coming out of the circus tent. "Welcome! I'm so happy to meet you! Let me introduce you to my grandson Bobby! He's going to perform on the trapeze—just as I did, when I was young!"

"Hello!" says Bobby. "My grandfather has told me a lot about you both! He says you're a newspaper photographer, Peter!"

"Maybe I'll get some shots of you for the paper!" says Peter.

Once they are seated, Aunt May begins to worry.

"Brad looks so happy," says Aunt May, "but he must really be sad! He's had lots of bad luck lately, and he must sell his circus!"

Before Peter can say anything, his spider-sense begins tingling! "Trouble's near!" thinks Peter to himself. "I must turn into Spider-Man!"

"Excuse me, Aunt May," says Peter. "I think I'll go and get us some popcorn and some soda!"

"All right, Peter!" says Aunt May.

Quick as a flash, Peter dashes into an empty tent and changes into Spider-Man.

"I wonder who would be mean enough to cause trouble in a circus?" thinks Spider-Man. "Could this person be the reason why Brad Steel must sell his circus? I'm going to stop this trouble before someone gets hurt!"

Everyone loves a parade—especially a circus parade! Everyone oohhs and ahhhs at the beautiful costumes. The audience laughs at the funny clowns. Everyone is amazed by all the big jungle animals! And there, on an elephant's back, is one of the stars of the show — little Bobby Steel!

But the biggest applause of all is given to the owner and ringmaster—the world famous performer, Brad Steel!

"Wow!" says Spidey, high above everyone. "Brad sure knows how to put on a great show!"

Suddenly, to everyone's horror, the lead elephant goes wild!

"Help!" screams the woman riding it. "I can't control Jumbo! Somebody do something!"

"Never fear, Spidey's here!" says Spidey, swinging down.

"I just hope I can stop him before he stampedes into the stands!" thinks Spidey.

"But how do you stop an elephant gone mad?" wonders Spidey. "Wait! What's that sticking out of the elephant's head?"

"Aha!" says Spidey. "This is what caused the elephant to go wild!"

And he quickly pulls a dart out of the elephant's forehead. Immediately, the elephant calms down.

"Hooray for Spidey!" everyone shouts.

"I wonder who shot this dart?" thinks Spidey.

Brad Steel motions for Spidey to come down beside him.

"Pretend it's all part of the show, Spidey, *please!*" whispers Brad. "I'll explain everything later—tonight, when everybody's gone!"

Spidey nods his head.

The audience roars it approval. Never before have they seen such a great stunt!

That night, Spidey enters the big top and sees Brad Steel waiting for him.

"Times have been tough, Spidey," says Brad. "I want Bobby to have a good life—go to college, make something of himself. But the circus is losing money. I thought putting it up for sale would solve my problems. But it just made them worse! Someone's trying to ruin me!"

"Don't worry, says Spidey. "I'll stop that madman— that's a promise!"

The next day is really special! The lion tamer is showing the big audience some new tricks he's taught his big cats!
"Nothing can happen now," thinks Spidey.
"All those lions are in cages!"

Suddenly the monkeys, lions, bears, giraffes—in fact, *all* the animals—start roaring and screaming in pain!

"Oh, no!" says Spidey. "Someone is using an ultra-sonic whistle that only animals and my spidey-senses can detect! It will drive them all wild!"

Before the lion tamer can get all the lions safely out of the big top, one of them breaks free!

"Look out! The lion is loose!" shout people in the audience. "Run! Run before he attacks us all!"

"Uh, oh!" says Spidey. "That lion is going to leap on that poor clown! I must stop the lion without hurting it!"

In an instant, Spidey leaps onto the lion's back.

"That was the easy part!" says Spidey. "Now to calm this big cat down! And I know just what to say!

"Nice kitty, good kitty. Everything will be all right."

As Spidey talks to the lion, the strange ultrasonic whistling stops and the lion calms down!

As the lion is peacefully lead back into his cage, Spidey looks around the big top.

"The danger is over for now," he says. "But the mean man who started this is still here! But where?"

Meanwhile, little Bobby Steel is climbing up the rope ladder leading to the trapeze.

"Come back, Bobby!" shouts his grandfather. "The trapeze is too dangerous!"

"No, it isn't, grandfather!" says Bobby. "I've practiced on it a thousand times! I know what I'm doing!"

"Someone is trying to destroy the circus—and he might hurt you!" shouts Brad Steel, but Bobby is too high to hear.

As Bobby nears the trapeze, Spidey is busy checking out the show.

"My spider-sense is not tingling, so everything is safe for now!" says Spidey. "Maybe my presence has scared away whoever was causing all the trouble."

"Things are rolling along really smoothly with you watching over us, Spidey!" says a clown.

"Let's hope it stays that way!" says Spidey. Then, he sees Bobby grabbing the trapeze. "Since everything has calmed down, I'm going to swing over and see Bobby's show!"

"Wow! Look at him go!" says Spidey, admiringly. "Bobby is great!"

And everyone else in the audience thinks so, too. They cheer louder than they've ever cheered before.

"I can see why Brad is so proud of his grandson," says Spidey.

At the end of his act, Bobby pauses to accept the applause. But just as he is about to grab the rope to go down to the ground, Spidey shouts, "Oh, no! My spider-sense is tingling like wild! Something bad is going to happen to Bobby!"

Suddenly, all the lights go out in the big top!

"Now I'll cut Bobby's rope! That should stop this show once and for all!" says a mysterious, mean voice.

"Yow!" shouts Bobby. "I'm falling! And there's no net below me! Help, Spider-Man! Help!"

"It's so dark. I'm blind as a
bat!" says Spidey. "But Bobby's
shout let me know where he was —
just in time! All I have to do is shoot out
my webbing and . . .
"I've got him!"
"Thank you, Spider-Man!" says Bobby. "You saved me!"

"Now to find the villain, once and for all!" says Spidey. And, turning on his belt beam, Spidey searches the entire tent. Suddenly, his Spider-light focuses on the clown that he saved from the lion! But that clown is holding a huge knife between his teeth!

"So *you're* the one who cut the rope!" shouts Spidey. "I know just what to do with you!"

In seconds, all the lights come on.

"Look, Spidey, my trick bike has spider-powers, too!" says the clown. "It can get around upside-down, just like you!"

"Hey, Spidey," asks Bobby. "What did you do with the clown who cut the rope?"

"Oh, him?" asks Spidey.

"I left him hanging," says Spidey, "over there!"

And, sure enough, there is the clown, dangling at the end of one of Spidey's sticky webs.

"Why did you cause all the trouble at the circus?" asks Spidey.

"I'm really sorry!" sobs the clown. "But, I loved this circus more than anything else in the world. And, when I heard Brad was going to sell it, I decided to do anything I could to stop anyone from wanting to buy it!"

"I love the circus, too," says Brad. "But what you did was wrong."

"I know that now," says the clown, as the police take him away.

Later that afternoon, Brad Steel's agent calls up.

"I've got great news!" says the agent. "Spider-Man got us so much publicity that everyone is interested in the circus! Your circus is booked solid for the next five years!"

"Yahoo!" shouts Brad. "That means I won't have to sell the circus!"

"Thank you for all your help, Spidey" says Brad.

"I'm always glad to lend a hand when it's needed most!" says Spidey. "Well, now that my job is done here, I'll be swinging off! See you soon!"

"Yes!" shout all the circus people. "Three cheers for Spidey! Hip Hip HOORAY!"